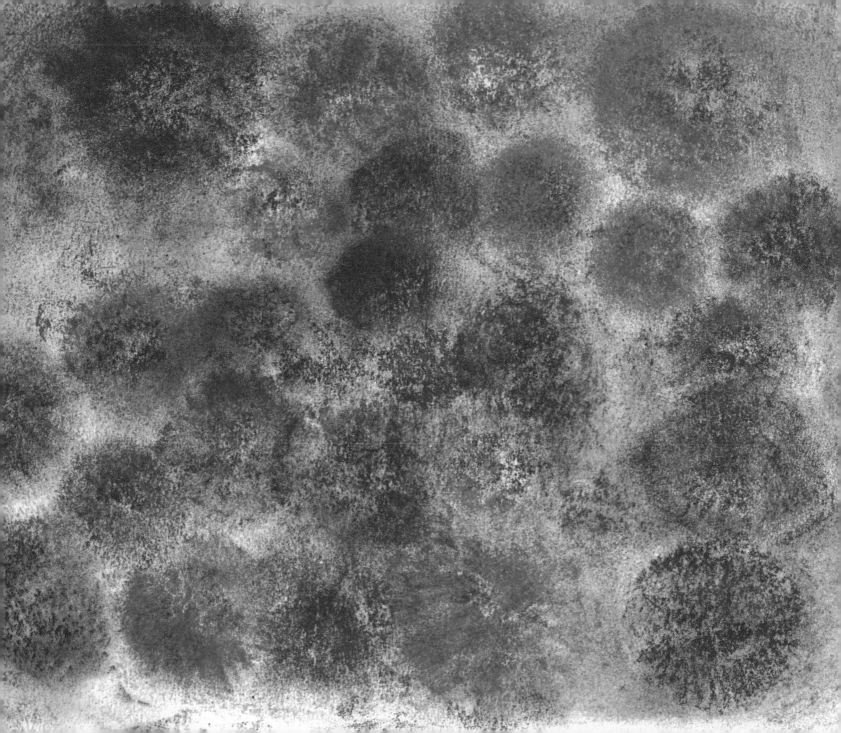

CHINESE EYES

Story by Marjorie Ann Waybill

Pauline Cutrell, Artist

HERALD PRESS

Scottdale, Pennsylvania **PRESS** **Kitchener, Ontario**

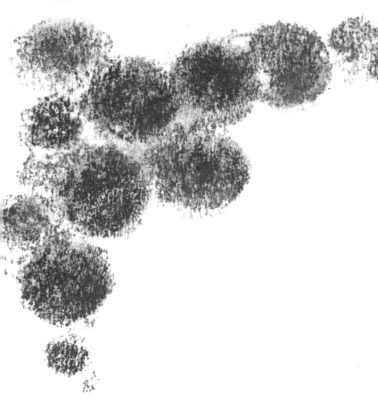

Library of Congress Cataloging in Publication Data

Waybill, Marjorie Ann, 1929-
  Chinese eyes.

    SUMMARY: An adopted Korean girl gets a lesson in
how unimportant it is that some people think she is
different.
    [1. Prejudices — Fiction] I. Cutrell, Pauline,
illus. II. Title.
PZ7.W35125Ch   [E]   74-5751
ISBN 0-8361-1738-7

CHINESE EYES

Copyright © 1974 by Herald Press, Scottdale, Pa. 15683
    Published simultaneously in Canada by Herald Press,
    Kitchener, Ont. N2G 4M5
Library of Congress Catalog Card Number: 74-5751
International Standard Book Number: 0-8361-1738-7
Printed in the United States of America
Design by Alice B. Shetler

82 83 84 85 86 87 88 89 10 9 8 7 6 5 4 3 2

To Peter, Steven, and Lois,
who inspired us to adopt
Becky, our little Chinese Eyes.

Becky's stomach told her it was lunchtime.
She looked up from her number paper to check
the big clock on the wall. Just then Miss Sager said,
"Time to line up for lunch, boys and girls."
Becky quickly put her number paper in her desk.
She asked Laura to get in line with her.

"Today we're having spaghetti," Becky whispered to Laura.

Laura rubbed her stomach. "I'm hungry enough to eat a thousand spaghettis!" she said. They both giggled.

"Let's go up the stairs more quietly today," Miss Sager said. "Yesterday we sounded like thunder on the steps. Maybe if we go quietly enough we can surprise the cooks!"

Becky liked Miss Sager. She had such good ideas.

The class tiptoed up the stairs to the cafeteria. Just as they came to the big serving window, Stuart sneezed! The head cook jumped! "I didn't hear you first-graders coming," she said.

Becky picked up her tray of food and went to the cafeteria. "I forgot today was ice-cream day," she said. She pulled the paper from her ice-cream bar. She always ate her ice cream first, before it got soft.

Lunchtime went
too fast. Becky pushed
her tray through the
cafeteria window. Then she
walked to the glass doors
to wait for Laura.

Two third-grade boys
came by on their way to
lunch. The tall, dark-haired
one turned and pointed
at her. "Hey, look!"
he said. "There's little
Chinese Eyes!" The others
turned to stare at her.

Becky didn't
know which way to
look. She just wanted
to hide her face.

"Hey, Becky," Laura called, "please wait for me."
She sipped the last drop of chocolate milk through the
straw. She wiped her mouth with the back of her
hand and came running over.

"Shall we play Hide the Thimble again?" Laura
asked.

Becky shook her head. She didn't want to play
with anyone. Not right now!

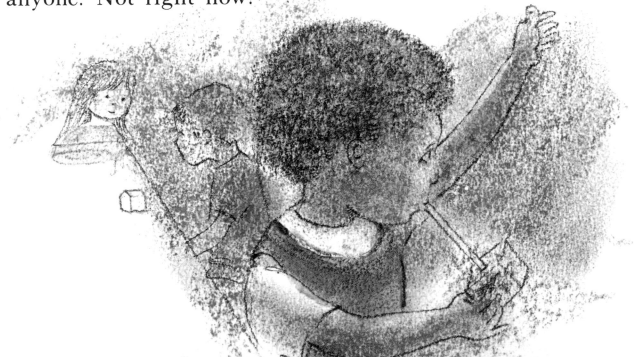

When they got back to the room, Becky went right to the playhouse. First she turned the sign on the roof to read "Do Not Disturb."

Then she crawled in the little door and sat on the carpet. Now no one could call her names. At least if they did, she couldn't hear them.

She put the earphones on
and pretended she was listening to records.
But she was thinking about Chinese eyes.

She couldn't understand it. That's exactly what the
boy at the park had called her. And those who heard
him laughed. Why did they say "Chinese eyes?" she
wondered. Mother said she had Korean eyes.

Becky was thinking so hard she almost forgot where she was. She peeked out of the little house and saw the other children in their seats.

She quickly hung the earphones on the peg beside the door and went to her seat.

It seemed the afternoon would never end. Nothing was going right. She made a mistake on her writing paper and had to start over. Once she leaned back too far on her chair and fell. Then her head hurt!

And when she came back from milk break Brian pointed at her orange, brown, and blue pants suit and sang, "Orange, brown, and blue makes a monkey out of you." Sometimes she laughed when he said that but not today. She pinched him instead.

Miss Sager saw her. "Becky," she said, "what seems to be the trouble?"

She couldn't answer. She was afraid if she opened her mouth to talk she would cry. So she just sat.

She wished she could kick Brian hard. She wished she could stand up and scream. She wished the last bell would ring. Just then it did ring.

"Good-bye, Becky," Miss Sager said as she squeezed her hand. Becky thought of asking Miss Sager about Chinese eyes. But she heard Laura calling her to come. Maybe she would ask Miss Sager about it tomorrow.

It was nice to be outdoors. The patrol boy helped Becky and Laura cross the street. Farther up the street, they saw Stuart waiting at the curb. "Hey," he yelled, "you promised to help me pick up nuts for my collection."

"I'd rather go home and get a drink first," said Laura. "My mouth is so dry it can't even sweat."

"Oh, come on. It won't take long if we hurry," Stuart begged.

So the three of them hurried over to the
big tree. Becky made a sack of her coat to
hold the nuts Laura and Stuart gathered.

She liked being with Laura and
Stuart. Laura was her very best
friend. Sometimes kids called
Laura ugly names. When they
did, Becky's stomach felt sick.
And it felt
sick today.

After they
had gathered the
nuts, they headed
down the street. Becky
cut across the empty
lot and was soon home.

"Hi, Becky," Mother called from the backyard."
"How about bringing me a good, cold drink?"

Becky found Mother by the big flowers. These were special flowers called dahlias. Mother had a name for each one. Becky's favorite was a big one called Santa Claus. It was red and white. Daddy liked the Moon Goddess. It was yellow. Mother's choice was the Black Narcissus because it was such a rare dahlia.

Becky and Mother
sat on the low stone
wall around the
flowers. "Did you
have a good day,
Becky?" Mother asked.

At first Becky
didn't answer. She
was thinking. Should
she tell Mother
about today?

"It was okay until lunchtime," Becky began. "But then some boy called me a name."

"What kind of name?" Mother asked. Becky sat quietly looking down at her feet. She didn't answer.

"People call each other all kinds of names," Mother said. "Sometimes they say, 'Slowpoke.' Sometimes they say, 'Fatty.' Sometimes they say, 'Cutie.' Did he call you any of those names?"

"No," Becky said as she looked up. "He called me 'Chinese Eyes.' "

Mother didn't seem shocked. She just said, "He was pretty close, wasn't he?"

Becky didn't know what she meant.

"Come indoors," Mother said, taking Becky by the hand. Mother laid the flowers on the kitchen table. "Now, you put the dahlias in a vase while I put my tools away."

"Okay, Becky," Mother said, returning to the kitchen. "Let's go look at ourselves in the big mirror." For a minute they stood looking. Then Mother said, "Can you see that my eyes are different from yours?"

Becky nodded. "You have blue eyes and mine are brown," she said. And then Becky noticed something else different. "Our eyes aren't shaped the same, either, are they?" she asked.

"No," Mother agreed. "But the children in China have eyes shaped like yours."

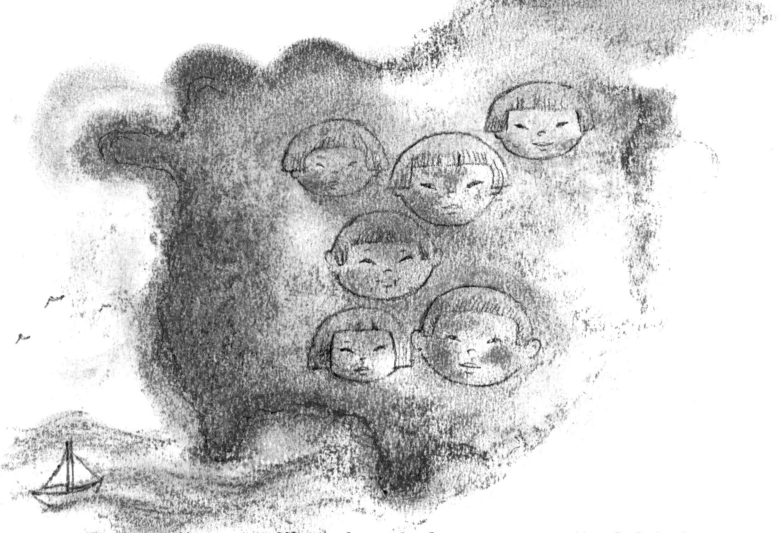

"CHINA?" Becky asked in surprise. "I didn't know there was a place called China." Suddenly she smiled all over. "They have Chinese eyes!" she exclaimed.

"And their eyes are beautiful," Mother added, "just like your eyes."

Becky smiled again. "But I know one way our eyes are alike," Becky said.

Mother thought a while. "How are they alike?" she asked.

"We can both see!" Becky exclaimed.

"Sure enough. You're right!" Mother said.

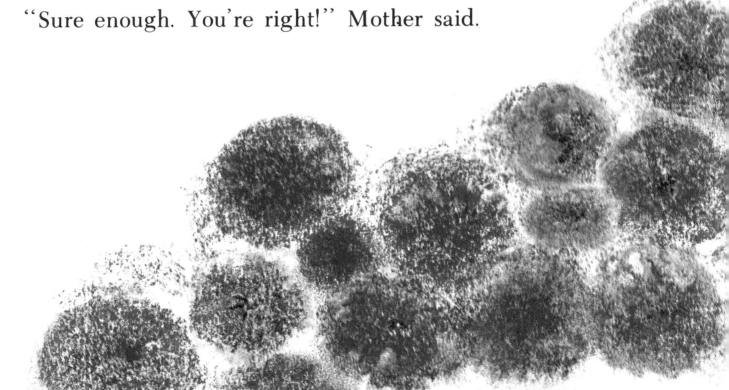

"I know something else," Mother said as she tapped Becky's nose.

"What's that?" Becky wondered.

"Well," Mother began, "you have a short nose and I have a long nose, but —"

"But," Becky giggled, "we can both smell the flowers!"

"You're right again!" Mother agreed.

Becky wrinkled her nose and they both laughed.

THE END

The Author

MARJORIE ANN WAYBILL has served as a substitute elementary teacher in the Southmoreland School District, Scottdale, Pennsylvania, since 1959. She taught for three years in a one-room school in Iowa. Later she taught second grade for two years in Indiana.

Mrs. Waybill was born near Middlebury, Indiana, and grew up on a farm near Kalona, Iowa. She received her BA degree in elementary education from Goshen College, Goshen, Indiana.

Her husband, Nelson, is a personnel manager. Their children are Peter Nelson, Steven Nelson, Lois Ann, and Rebecca Ann.

Becky, the leading character in this book, came to the Waybill home from Korea through Holt Adoption Program, Inc., Eugene, Oregon. She was almost two when she joined her new family on December 13, 1967.

The Artist

PAULINE CUTRELL is a free-lance illustrator of children's periodicals and curriculum who lives near Scottdale, Pennsylvania.